Be A Good Sport, Diggory Doo!
My Dragon Books - Volume 47
Written by Steve Herman

ISBN: 978-1-64916-110-9 (paperback)
ISBN: 978-1-64916-111-6 (hardcover)

www.MyDragonBooks.com

First Edition: August 2021
10 9 8 7 6 5 4 3 2 1

Diggory's in a chess club –
it's his favorite game to play –
He's good and almost always wins,
but much to my dismay,

Diggory wasn't nice when playing well
and winning games;
He laughed at his opponents
and even called them names!

But whenever Diggory lost,
you could hear his awful roar!

When Diggory Doo plays soccer,
he's really hard to beat;
He scores a lot of goals;
he's got talent in his feet!

Diggory always took the credit
for his team's success,
But when Diggory's team was losing?
Look out! What a mess!

Although Diggory plays real well,
sometimes he made mistakes,

But blamed them on his teammates –
That's not fair for goodness' sakes!

"Winning is the only thing that matters," Diggory said –

But when the other team was winning, Diggory Doo saw red!

Diggory stomped his foot
and argued with the referee;

"Whenever you win a game, you brag that you're the best; Have you thought how that makes others feel?" – "I haven't," he confessed.

"And when you're playing soccer,
you may score a goal or two,
But you seem to have forgotten,
someone kicked the ball to you."

"Winning isn't everything,
so Diggory you must learn
There is more to winning
than how many points you earn."

"Like when someone else does better than you in playing chess, You can say, 'Congratulations! Good job!' or 'You're the best!'"

"Although you like to be first place, remember, Diggory Doo –
You like how it feels to win; let others feel it, too."

Diggory listened carefully
and took my words to heart –
The next time we played soccer,
he had made a brand new start.

"But no one saw it happen,"
was our disappointed cry;
"But I know, and that's what matters,"
was Diggory Doo's reply.

The game went into overtime;
we played with all our might –
In the end, we lost the game,
but Diggory Doo was right.

"We like to win," we said,
"but we like playing more
Now that Diggory Doo plays nicer
than he ever did before."

Now when Diggory Doo is winning,
he doesn't brag or boast,
And no tantrums when he's losing –
He knows what matters most –

COLLECT THEM ALL!

Visit www.MyDragonBooks.com for more!!!